THE OFFICIAL CRAZY BONES® COLLECTOR'S GUIDE

SCHOLASTIC INC.
New York   Toronto   London   Auckland   Sydney
Mexico City   New Delhi   Hong Kong

If you purchased this book without a cover, you should be aware that this book is stolen property. It was reported as "unsold and destroyed" to the publisher, and neither the author nor the publisher has received payment for this "stripped book."

No part of this publication may be reproduced in whole or in part, or stored in a retrieval system, or transmitted in any form or by any means, electronic, mechanical, photocopying, recording, or otherwise, without written permission of the publisher. For information regarding permission, write to Permissions Department, Scholastic Inc., 555 Broadway, New York, NY 10012.

ISBN 0-439-15403-0

CRAZY BONES ® characters © MAGIC BOX INT'L 1996; © 2000 MAGIC BOX INT'L, All Rights Reserved; ® and © designate properties of MAGIC BOX INT'L and/or TOY CRAZE and are used under license by Scholastic Inc. All rights reserved. Published by Scholastic Inc.

12 11 10 9 8 7 6 5 4 3 2 1   0 1 2 3 4 5 6/0

Printed in the U.S.A.
First Scholastic printing, January 2000
Book design: Michael Malone

THE OFFICIAL CRAZY BONES COLLECTOR'S GUIDE

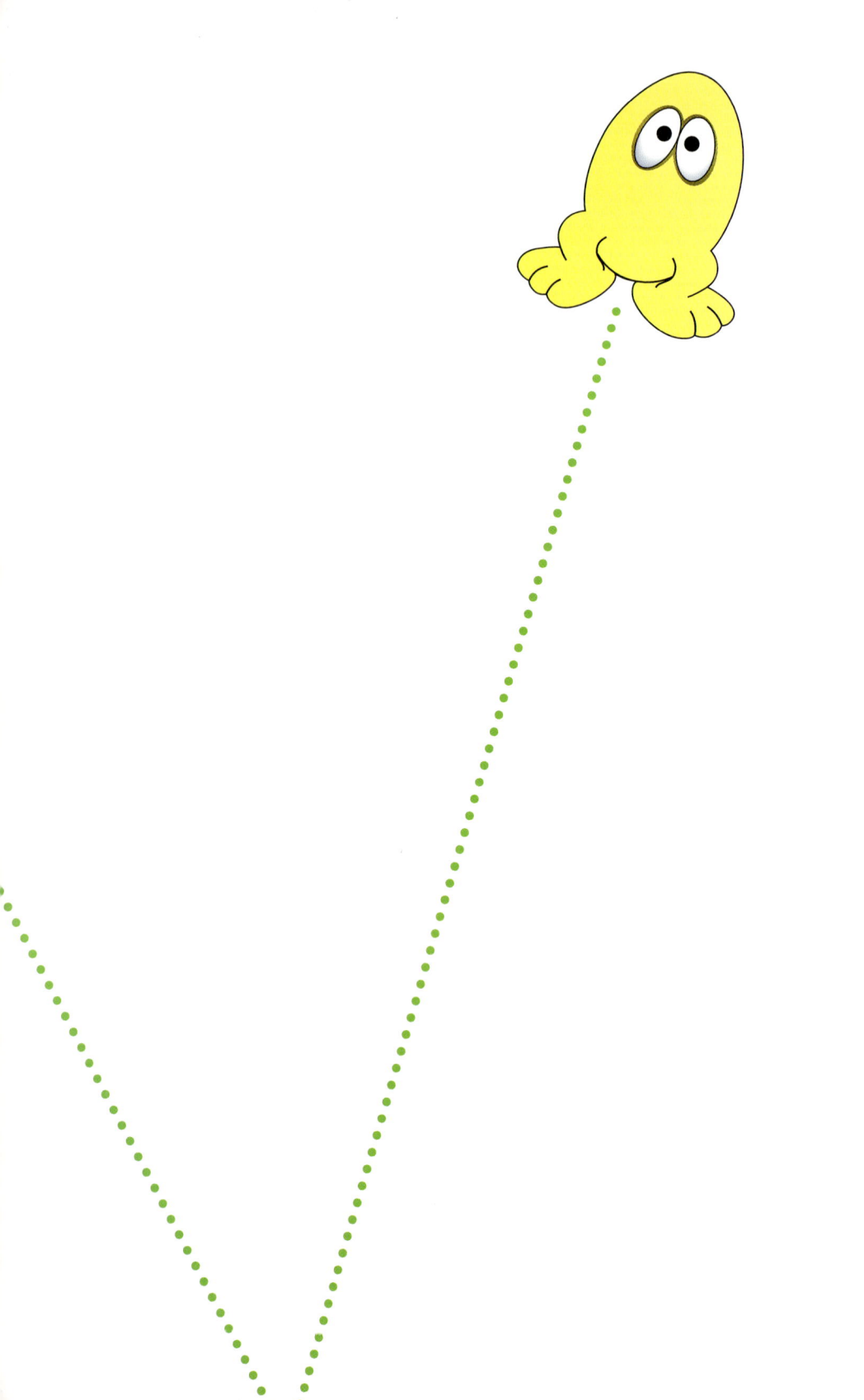

Table of Contents

The Bone Zone 6
In the Beginning 8
Colors and Styles 10
Collecting Tips 12
Retired Bones 14
Ask Webster! 16
Fun & Bones 20
The Go-Go's 26
Things 41
Sports 56
Buddies 66
The Alien Invasion! 82
Aliens 85
Play Crazy Games! 94

Crazy Bones are cool. Crazy Bones are hip. Crazy Bones are, well, crazy—and they're the hottest thing to hit town since neon hula hoops.

What's that, you ask? What are Crazy Bones?

If you don't already know, then what are you doing with this book?! Okay, listen up. We'll say this just once:

Crazy Bones are wacky,
nutty, goofy, wild characters
that come in dozens
of colors, shapes, and styles.
They are cool to collect.
Terrific to trade!
And totally awesome
to play with!
So get crazy.
Get Crazy Bones!
Start your collection today.
You'll love 'em.
Really.
We're talking love.
A dozen red roses.
A heart-shaped box of chocolates.
That kind of love.
No?
Okay, you'll really like 'em.
A lot.

GET THE REAL DEAL...
Beware of cheap, rotten imitations! The genuine Crazy Bones are only made for Toy Craze, Inc. by Magic Box International. Look at the back of your Crazy Bones and you will see the official logo. The logo of Magic Box International is your guarantee that your item is genuine and of the highest quality. Don't be fooled by imitations. Demand the real deal.

IN THE BEGINNING

Crazy Bones may be the latest craze, but it's far from the newest thing to hit town. In fact, the children of ancient Rome and Greece played with toys that inspired the creation of modern Crazy Bones.

Imagine this: It's about two thousand years ago. There are few kids sitting around, trying to decide what to do. Should they play Sony PlayStation? Go to the ramps and catch "big air" on their computerized skateboards? Or just lie around watching MTV?

NOT!

So somebody gets a bright idea. (Okay, maybe it's a gross idea, but never mind that.) Maybe there are a few dead sheep lying around, doing nothing (as dead sheep are wont to do). Maybe there are a few bones left out in the sun. So this Roman kid with a high IQ looks at the bones, specifically the sheep's knuckles, and gets a crazy idea. He (or she) decides to paint the bones. And then, before you know it, everybody's doing it. Kids and grown-ups alike. Gathering bones. Decorating bones. Making up bone games. Sounds crazy, right?

Well, we're pretty sure of one thing. The sheep weren't too thrilled with the idea. What follows is an actual transcript of an actual conversation between two actual sheep in Rome, about 2,126 years ago, just before lunch:

Sheep #1: "Did you see what happened to my cousin Dave?"
Sheep #2: "Yeah, he died a few weeks ago. I told him not to eat that sandal."
Sheep #1: "That's not the worst of it."
Sheep #2: "It gets worse than death?"
Sheep #1: "Around here it does. First these kids came along and took his knuckles."

Sheep #2: "So, big deal. He was dead already. It's not like he needed those knuckles."
Sheep #1: "Still, it's gross. I mean, how would you like it if somebody decided to play with your knuckle bones?"
Sheep #2: "I see your point. What do they do with the knuckles anyway? Make knuckle sandwiches?"
Sheep #1: "Worse. They paint the bones and bounce them all over the place. It's crazy."
Sheep #2: "Poor Dave."
Sheep #1: "You can say that again."
Sheep #2: "Poor Dave."
Sheep #1: "Oh, shut up!"

Okay. The truth is, we made that conversation up. In fact, we have no idea what sheep talked about in Rome two thousand years ago. Come to think of it, they probably just talked about grass.

Sheep #1: "Yum. Grass is tasty today."
Sheep #2: "Delicious."
Sheep #1: "So green and sweet."
Sheep #2: "Nutritious."
Sheep #1: "Look at me."
Sheep #2: "Huh? What?"
Sheep #1: "Look at me. Do I have any grass stuck between my teeth?"

So, sure. Sheep are kind of dull. Anyway, a lot of time passed. Minutes, hours, hundreds and hundreds of years. The ancient game was suddenly revived in Spain in 1996. Don't worry, sensitive reader, today's Crazy Bones aren't made of sheep's knuckles. Actually, they're made of modern space-age materials—okay, sure, plastic—and, holy cow, can they bounce! Bing, zing, they are outta here! Plus, the modern Crazy Bones feature all kinds of wild, nutty, goofy characters. What could be more fun than that?!

SHEEP DON'T GET ANY RESPECT.

Colors & Styles

Each individual Crazy Bone comes in a variety of types and colors. There are Glowies and Jellies, Sparkles and Toothpaste, Gooies, Metals, Ice Bones, and Whistlers! Here's a quick guide to help you know the difference.

Glowies

These Crazy Bones actually glow in the dark!

Ice Bones

Transparent in appearance, molded to perfection.

Precious Metals (Gold)

Gold Crazy Bones are extremely rare. In fact, they are considered the rarest among all Crazy Bones!

Metals

These silver and bronze metals are considered rare, yet still attainable.

Jellies

Clear, softly-colored Bones have a soothing appearance.

Other Bones (not shown)

Toothpaste
Swirls of colors mixed with streams of pearly white.

Gooies
Melted differently into a unique — and gooey — Bone shape.

Whistlers
Pick up one of these Bones and blow into the hole like a soda bottle.

Sparkles
Speckled with silver and gold dust throughout. They are easily recognizable when placed side by side with other Bones.

Collecting Tips

There are three essential rules to remember when collecting Crazy Bones. These rules are very, very important, so I've asked the book designer to set the rules in LARGE TYPE. Please read the following rules slowly, and repeat them out loud. Are you ready?

Rule #1: HAVE FUN!

Rule #2: HAVE FUN!

Rule #3: HAVE FUN!

Have you got the idea? Collecting Crazy Bones isn't a science and it's certainly not a competition. It's a way for you and your friends—new and old—to get together and, well, have fun.

The thing about collecting is that you don't have to buy a million packs of Crazy Bones. The fastest, cheapest, friendliest way to collect is to trade.

Most collectors start out by trying to complete a series. You might want to collect all of the Go-Go's or all of the Aliens. Later on, if you wish, you can try to collect a complete set of a certain type. That could be a complete set of glow-in-the-dark Go-Go's. Or you can focus on one character, collecting different colors and styles.

The real trick is...have fun!

Trading Tips

1. Make a checklist of all the Crazy Bones you have.

2. Keep one of everything in a safe place. These are the Crazy Bones you want to keep. Often when trading, collectors can get caught up in the excitement. Then you might make a trade that you'll later regret.

3. Put all your duplicates in one place. These are the Crazy Bones that you can trade. If you've got two Bikers, for example, you should decide which one you want to keep...and which one to trade.

4. Take one of your duplicates and show it to your fellow collectors. You might say, "Does anyone need an Eggy?" When you find someone who wants one of your duplicates, look at your own checklist. Which characters do you need? If there's a match, then go ahead and make the trade.

5. Remember, in a trade, everyone should be happy. No one loses. Both people in a trade should walk away happy, and that much closer to completing their collection!

Retired Bones

You know how when grown-ups get older, they retire from their jobs? They work for years and years and finally—finally!—they stop working. Then they relax, take sea cruises, play shuffleboard, and maybe even start a little hobby—like building bird houses in the basement, or knitting eight-foot-long scarves.

Same thing with Crazy Bones.

Okay. Not exactly.

Okay, okay. It's not at all the same thing! Not even close. But Crazy Bones do retire. Really.

For example, Toy Craze (the fabulous company that makes Crazy Bones in the United States), stopped production of the original sixty characters, known and loved as "The Go-Go's."

The molds have been broken. No more will be made. In the words of Toy Craze, they've been "buried." What does that mean? The Go-Go's are Gone-Gone. You can't buy them anymore.

It also means that they will become rare, hard to find. Just the kind of thing that a collector seeks, because rare things increase in value. So if you've got a glow-in-the-dark Eggy lying around, hold on to it! That little guy is nearly impossible to find anymore! As time goes on, new Crazy Bones will be introduced. And, yes, old ones will be retired. After all, they like to play shuffleboard, too!

ALSO BURIED
Hold on to any Crazy Bones that are black, white, or brown. They've been buried, too!

STICK WITH CRAZY BONES®
(and Crazy Bones will stick with you!)

Each Crazy Bones character has its very own sticker. Collect them all in a special sticker album!

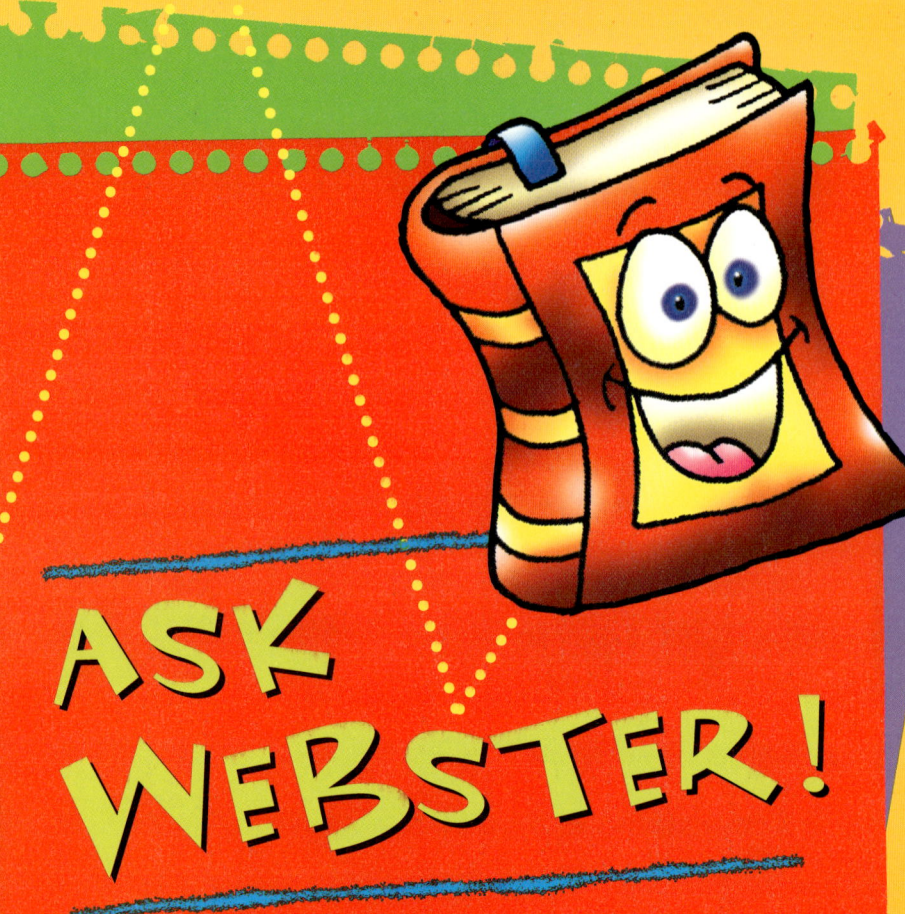

ASK WEBSTER!

Which is the most valuable Crazy Bone?
Although some Crazy Bones are harder to find than others, like Gold Bones, they are all worth the same amount. What makes a Crazy Bone valuable is how much *you* value it!

Which are the rarest Crazy Bones?
The rarest of the Crazy Bones are definitely the Gold Bones. There is only about one Gold Bone for every thousand Crazy Bones.

What are the most valuable colors?
Although all Crazy Bones are worth the same amount of money, there are three colors that have been retired. That makes Bones in those colors much harder to find. The colors are black, white and brown.

Who thought of Crazy Bones?
Crazy Bones were invented by a man named José Bella in Spain. One day José was in a museum with his kids and saw pieces from a game called Tabas that was played by children in ancient times. Kids painted faces on the dried knucklebones of sheep and played with them like dice or marbles. Since the bones would have bounced in crazy ways José called his new game Crazy Bones.

How do you get good at Crazy Bones games?
Practice, practice, practice!

How many Crazy Bones are there?
There are over 200 different Crazy Bones characters, and more are on the way.

Which are the best Crazy Bones for games?
Usually the best characters are the ones that are the roundest without many parts that stick out. Speedy is great because he is almost completely round and rolls and bounces straight. E.T. is not very good at games because his eyes stick out so much he doesn't roll or bounce predictably.

Where can I get the latest information on Crazy Bones?

Go to the official Crazy Bones Web site at www.crazybones.com. You'll find up-to-the-minute information, including new ways to "Play the Craze!" Plus, you'll find exciting interactive activities and contests offering Crazy Bones prizes. Most important, there's a special area that helps you trade with other Crazy Bones-loving computer users. Take a look at what you'll find!

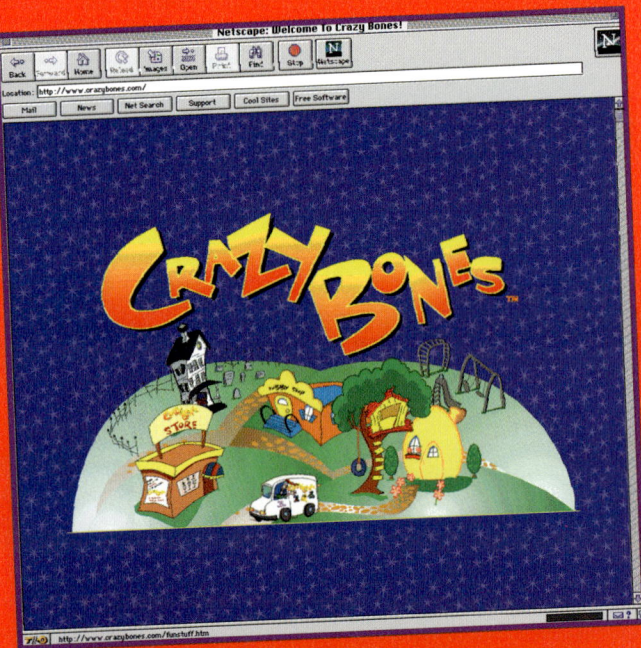

All sorts of options to explore...

including trading opportunities...

cool things to buy...

Crazy Bone profiles...

and much more!

Fun & Bones

Just for fun, we got all the Crazy Bones together and asked them*
for a list of their favorite movies, books, athletes, television shows—
and so on. Their replies were so rip-roaringly funny we decided
to share them with you, dear reader.

Okay, okay. We made the whole thing up!

CRAZY BONES AT THE MOVIES!

Crazy Bone	Favorite Movie
Orby	Around the World in 80 Days
Mumma Mia	The Mummy
Martian	My Favorite Martian
Space Frog	The Muppets in Outer Space
Tarzalien	George of the Jungle
Ghost	Beetlejuice
Vampire	Dracula
Creature	Godzilla
Lucas	Star Wars
Puppy	Beethoven
Hunchbone	The Hunchback of Notre Dame
Oink	Babe
Puck	The Mighty Ducks
Rat Fink	Mouse Hunt
Squat	Honey, I Shrunk the Kids
Hulk	Hercules
Brains	Flubber

I'D GIVE IT TWO THUMBS UP... IF I HAD ANY THUMBS!

CRAZY BONES AT THE LIBRARY

Crazy Bone — **Author: Favorite Book**

Eggy .... Dr. Seuss: *Horton Hatches the Egg*
Ma Kettle .... Maurice Sendak: *Chicken Soup With Rice*
Bookworm .... Eric Carle: *The Very Hungry Caterpillar*
Cowboy .... Lynne Reid Banks: *The Indian in the Cupboard*
Webster .... Donald Sobol: *Encyclopedia Brown*
Fudgy .... Judy Blume: *Superfudge*
Artist .... Tomie dePaola: *The Art Lesson*
Snooze .... Graeme Base: *The Eleventh Hour*
Rapper .... Bill Martin, Jr: *Chicka Chicka Boom Boom*
Surprise .... Clement Clark Moore: *The Night Before Christmas*
Chef .... Roald Dahl: *Charlie and the Chocolate Factory*
Biker .... Beverly Cleary: *The Mouse and the Motorcycle*
Pig Tails .... Beverly Cleary: *Ramona the Brave*
Brains .... David Macaulay: *The Way Things Work*
Snippy .... Gary Paulsen: *Hatchet*
Miss Froggy .... Arnold Lobel: *Frog and Toad Are Friends*
Tarzalien .... Chris Van Allsburg: *Jumanji*
Bug Eye .... Bruce Coville: *My Teacher Is an Alien*

CRAZY BONES ON THE BOOB TUBE!

Crazy Bone	Favorite Television Show
Puppy	"Scooby-Doo"
Bikini Baby	"The Powerpuff Girls"
Karate	"Kung Fu"
Speedy	"Speed Racer"
Baby	"Rugrats"
Fly Boy	"The Adventures of Superman"
Dopey	"Dumb Bunnies"
Sheriff Bones	"The Lone Ranger"
S.O.S.	"Gilligan's Island"
Bug Eye	"Men in Black"
Goodie Goodie	"Happy Days"
Stretcher	"E.R."
Coach	"Coach"
Time Out	"The Big Comfy Couch"
Tentacle	"SpongeBob SquarePants"

CRAZY BONES ON THE RADIO!

Crazy Bone	Recording Artist: Song
Olé	Ricky Martin: "Livin' La Vida Loca"
Champ	Queen: "We Are the Champions"
Cowboy	Will Smith: "Wild Wild West"
Striker	Smash Mouth: "All Star"
Punk	The Ramones: "Sheena Is a Punk Rocker"
Bootz	Nancy Sinatra: "These Boots Are Made for Walking"
Shady	Madonna: "Ray of Light"
S.O.S	The Beatles: "Help"
Pouch	The Box Tops: "The Letter"
Jaws	The Beach Boys: "Surfin' U.S.A."
Babe	Britney Spears: "(You Drive Me) Crazy"

CRAZY BONES AND THEIR FAVORITE ATHLETES

I LOVE HIS HAIR.

HE'S GOT A GREAT NICKNAME.

SHE SHOULD MEET EGGY.

HE'S FROM MY HOME PLANET.

BALDY	MAC	OINK	TRI-CLOPS
MICHAEL JORDAN	MARK McGWIRE	MIA HAMM	DENNIS RODMAN

QUICKIE QUIZ

What's Ghost's favorite band?
The Backsheet Boys.

What's Bully's favorite vegetable?
Black-eyed peas.

What's Time Out's favorite snack?
Couch potato chips.

What's Ma Kettle's favorite song?
"Home on the Range."

What's Hooray's favorite drink?
Root beer.

What's Stinky's favorite band?
'N Stink!

What's Tubby's favorite place to eat?
Anywhere!

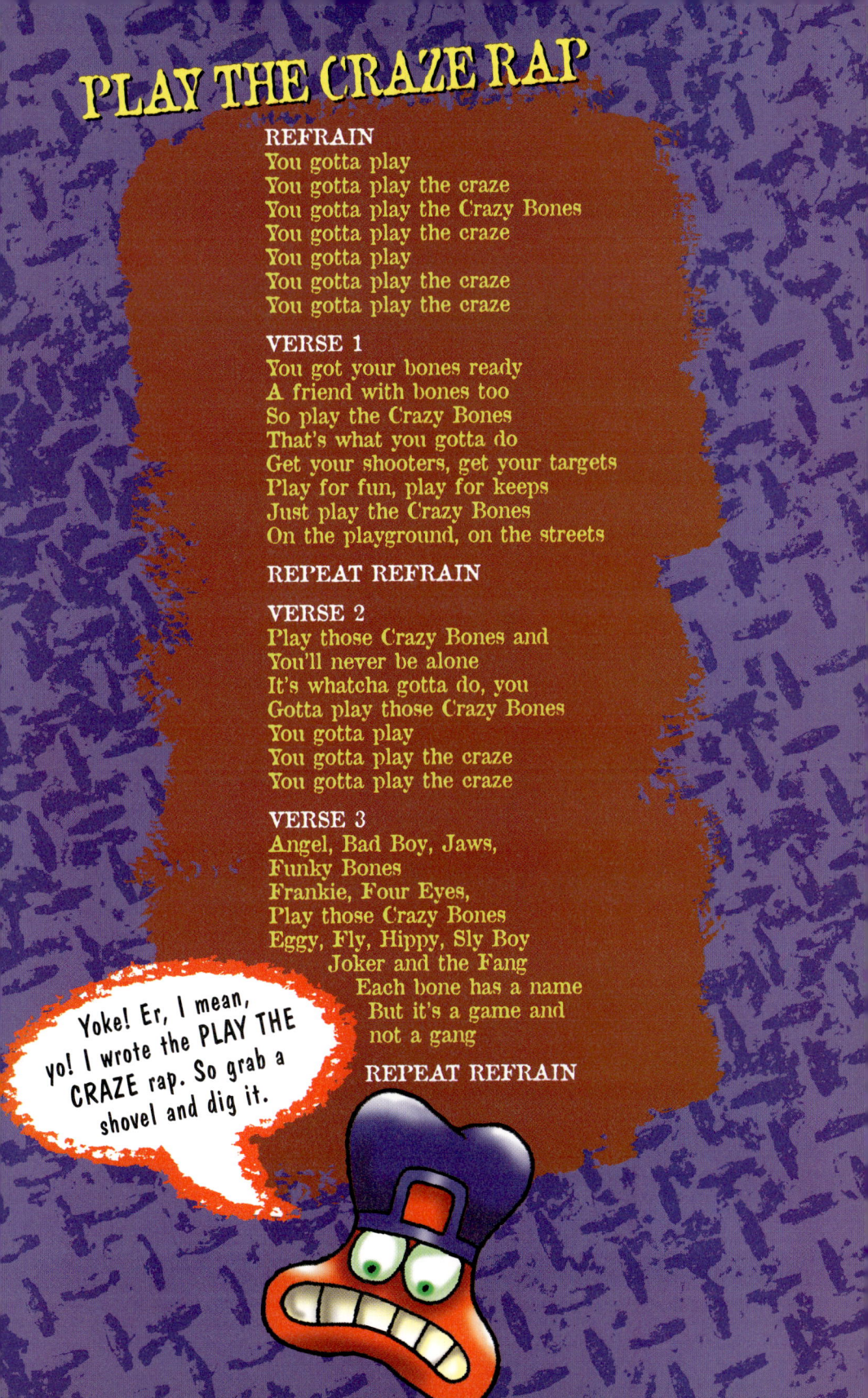

"THE GO-GO'S"

1. Music

"I love to put on my headphones and jam all day."

2. Smiley

"Hey, check out these pearly whites!"

3. Eggy

"I'm the main man of the Crazy Bones clan."

4. Hippy

"Give peace a chance."

"THE GO-GO'S"

5. Vampire

"This book is driving me batty."

6. Daydreamer

"Excuse me? Did you say something? I was busy daydreaming."

7. Weirdo

"My parents are Mr. and Mrs. Normal. So what happened to me?"

8. Wow

"My dog's name is Bow-Wow."

"THE GO-GO'S"

9. Biker

"Who says I need a shave?!"

10. Menace

"I'm like Dennis — only a little worse."

11. Punk

"I'm the lead singer of a punk rock group, The Punkadelics."

12. Junior

"Excuse me, is my hair on fire?"

"THE GO-GO'S"

13. Baldy

"I've got a lock on my nose. Don't try to pick it."

14. Funny Bone

"You know me. I'm connected to the elbow bone."

15. Heavy Metal

"I like my music loud — and really, really dumb."

16. The Fly

"What's the buzz?"

"THE GO-GO'S"

17. Rocker

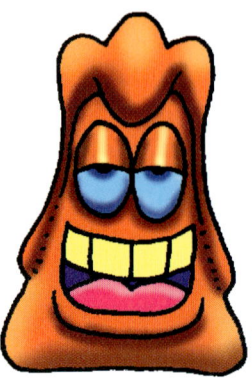

"I play drums for the Punkadelics."

18. Top Hat

"It's not hard being green."

19. Rapper

"I wrote the Crazy Bones Rap, PLAY THE CRAZE."

20. Sweetie

"I'm sweeter than sugar and twice as nice."

"THE GO-GO'S"

21. Grumpy

"Yuck! Another rotten day!"

22. Ghost

"I'm so scary, sometimes I even scare myself."

23. E.T.

"Phone home? Forget that. I send e-mail!"

24. Goodie Goodie

"I'm telling."

"THE GO-GO'S"

25. Bone Jour

"Vive la France!"

26. Long John

"Walk the plank, landlubbers!"

27. Big Mouth

"Blab, blab, blab."

28. Chef

"Hey everybody, what's cooking?"

"THE GO-GO'S"

29. Reggae

"Come to the Islands, man."

30. Babe

"Is my lipstick on straight?"

31. Four Eyes

"I have double vision."

32. Cowboy

"I love country and western music."

"THE GO-GO'S"

33. James Bone

"I've got a license to thrill."

34. Jaws

"I love swimmers. They're delicious."

35. Scared

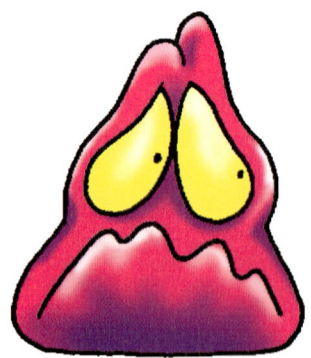

"I'm scared of everything—especially Jaws and Frankie!"

36. Frankie

"Let's do the Monster Mash!"

"THE GO-GO'S"

37. Screamer

"I scream so loud, I should be in a horror flick."

38. Dummy

"Aren't I bit old for a pacifier?"

39. Clown

"I love cotton candy and peanuts...for breakfast!"

40. Monster

"For me, every day is Halloween."

"THE GO-GO'S"

41. Cool Dude

"I'm so cool, if I were a thing I'd be a refrigerator."

42. Pig Tails

"Life is one giant pep rally. Go, team, GO!"

43. Dreamer

"People say I've got my head in the clouds."

44. Sly Boy

"It's not cheating if you don't get caught."

"THE GO-GO'S"

45. Joker

"Did you hear about the boneless chicken? It only lays scrambled eggs!"

46. Speedy

"When I feel the need, I go for speed."

47. Fang

"Fangs for the memories."

48. Nice Guy

"A good deed a day keeps the doctor away."

"THE GO-GO'S"

49. Teacher's Pet

"I love sharpening pencils."

50. Tubby

"At least they don't call me CHUBBY."

51. Scary

"My favorite thing? Sneaking up on Scared and yelling, 'BOO!'"

52. Brains

"If I'm so smart, why am I wearing this goofy bow tie?"

"THE GO-GO'S"

53. Freddie Frog

"What's wrong with blue and slimy?"

54. Sleepy

"Zzzzzz."

55. New Wave

"Fashion is my passion."

56. Bad Boy

"When me and Menace get together — watch out!"

"THE GO-GO'S"

57. Dopey

"Uh, er, I don't know nothing."

58. Angel

"Helping others is what life's all about."

59. Chubby

"At least they don't call me TUBBY."

60. Miss Froggy

"Let's go to the hop!"

"THINGS"

61. Crazy Bug

"My grandfather is a VW station wagon."

62. Snippy

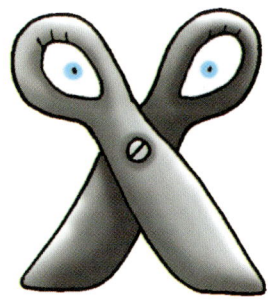

"I'm on the cutting edge."

63. Inky

"Write on!"

64. Ma Kettle

"Have a little soup. It's good for you."

"THINGS"

65. Artist

"My favorite artist is Vincent Van Bone."

66. Pssst

"Don't blame me for the hole in the ozone layer!"

67. Bootz

"This Bootz is made for walking."

68. Spinner

"Let me clean up your act!"

"THINGS"

69. Jammer

"You turn me on."

70. Edison

"I'm brighter than your average bulb."

71. Graham Bone

"Rotary rocks!"

72. Twist

"I'm a pencil sharpener, in case you didn't notice!"

"THINGS"

73. Carmen Boneranda

"A pineapple a day keeps the dentist away."

74. Surprise

"It's a wrap!"

75. Toasty

"Is it getting warm in here, or is it me?"

76. Veggie

"Cauliflower Power!"

"THINGS"

77. Can Can

"Yes, I can-can. No, you can't-can't."

78. Java

"Let's face it. Life can be a grind."

79. Bone Bag

"Hey, I heard that. I do NOT look like a sack of potatoes!"

80. Corked

"You should meet my pop."

"THINGS"

81. Mac

"Big Mac is my favorite baseball slugger. Go figure."

82. Flash

"Go. Stop! Go. Stop! Go. Stop! I can never make up my mind."

83. Champ

"I love myself. Hey, somebody's got to!"

84. Comfy

"Relax. Kick off your shoes. Take it easy."

"THINGS"

85. Giga Bone

"Come closer. I won't byte."

86. Nutty

"How do you like my new threads?"

87. Sandy

"I like timing Eggy."

88. Chester

"I was voted Best Dresser in my class."

"THINGS"

89. Snooze

"Alarming, aren't I?"

90. Miss T.

"I'm really steamed."

91. Frenchy

"I'm fast food. Want to race?"

92. Webster

"Got a question? Ask Webster!"

"THINGS"

93. Bone Cone

"I scream for ice cream!"

94. Type-O

"I guess you could say I'm a little old-fashioned."

95. Sprinkles

"I never met a flower I didn't like."

96. Swirly

"I was born in Flushing, New York."

"THINGS"

97. Petals

"My real name is Daisy."

98. Ringo

"The beat goes on!"

99. Shady

"I hate it when I forget my sunglasses."

100. Pouch

"Can you guess whether I'm mail or femail?"

"THINGS"

101. Topper

"Anyone care to dance the funky chicken?"

102. S.O.S.

"No one drowns when I'm around!"

103. Weighty

"I used to be heavy. But I scaled down."

104. Olé

"Livin' La Vida Loca, baby!"

"THINGS"

105. Combo

"You're safe with me."

106. Slurp

"Good to the last slurp!"

107. Fudgy

"No, you can't eat my cherry!"

108. Vendo

"It's a mystery to me."

"THINGS"

109. Planet Go-Go

"Out of this world!"

110. Piggy

"I'll never change."

111. Nautilus

"Hey, could you give me a lift?"

112. Screwy

"And you thought Nutty was weird!"

"THINGS"

113. Nimble

"What's with Jack? Did he swallow Mexican jumping beans or something?!"

114. Orby

"All my life's a circle."

115. Squeeze

"Watch it, that TICKLES!"

116. Octo Bone

"There are many sides to my personality."

"THINGS"

117. Rubbish

"I love talking trash."

118. Cable Guy

"31 channels. Still nothing on."

119. Melon Head

"If I had arms, then I'd have armpits!"

120. Nitro

"5-4-3-2-1. Blast off!"

"SPORTS"

1. Champ

"The winner gets me!"

2. Flash

"Say 'cheese'!"

3. Fan

"Front row seats. Awesome!"

4. Play-by-Play

"And now for another commercial."

"SPORTS"

5. Cry Baby

"I've got to stop eating so many onions."

6. Scarfo

"Does this match my outfit?"

7. Yikes

"I worry about everything."

8. Hooray

"I invented the Wave! Surf's up!"

"SPORTS"

9. Coach

"Sometimes, late at night, I pray for eyelids."

10. Banger

"Let's get LOUD!"

11. Commish

"Just call me Boss."

12. Ball

"Want to play?"

"SPORTS"

13. Net

"Uh-oh. That guy can really kick."

14. Stretcher

"I'll pick you up when you're feeling down."

15. Cleats

"Traction is my main action."

16. Corner Kick

"Every day is Flag Day when I'm around."

"SPORTS"

17. O.T.

"I hate time-outs."

18. Horn

"When I honk, players listen."

19. Handy

"I'm a soccer player with hands. Terrific."

20. Footskills

"It doesn't matter to me if I'm up or down."

"SPORTS"

21. P.K.

"I love penalty kicks."

22. Free Kick

"This is where the fun starts!"

23. Winner

"How do you like my new hat?"

24. Mr. Cool

"I'm the coolest Crazy Bone on the field."

"SPORTS"

25. The Kid

"Hey, don't call me Sonny!"

26. Center

"I'm the man in the middle."

27. Rookie

"Whoops!"

28. Header

"I always use my head."

"SPORTS"

29. Dynomite

"When I play, it's a blast!"

30. Keeper

"Nobody scores when I'm around."

31. Trash Talk

"Actually, I believe in recycling."

32. Hacker

"I'm a mean, lean, hacking machine."

"SPORTS"

33. D•Rex

"You think I'm tough? You should meet my cousin T. Rex."

34. Cheap Shot

"I never met a foul I didn't like."

35. Wheels

"I'm faster than a speeding soccer ball."

36. Head Case

"It's hard to find a hat my size."

"SPORTS"

37. Nut Meg

"I add spice to every game."

38. Striker

"Scoring goals is what I do."

39. Silly

"Look at me, look at me! Yowsa!"

40. Shag

"Who turned out the lights?"

"BUDDIES"

1. Tin Man

"Hey, I've got a lotta heart!"

2. Robo

"I run on two AA batteries."

3. Rosey

"I'll clean houses. But I don't do windows."

4. Stewie

"I smell home cooking!"

"BUDDIES"

5. Shades

"I am stylin' in these sunglasses."

6. Squat

"I'm not short, I'm just afraid of heights."

7. Overbite

"I can open tin cans with these babies!"

8. Oink

"It's swine time!"

"BUDDIES"

9. Grad

"I graduated summa cum Bon-a."

10. Pudge

"At least they don't call me CHUBBY."

11. Puck

"Hockey rules!"

12. Eel

"What a shock — I'm electric."

"BUDDIES"

13. Stash

"Actually, it's not a mustache. It's just very long nose hair."

14. Wooly

"I'm tired of scrubbing things. I just want to dance."

15. Jester

"Anybody want to clown around?"

16. Hard Hat

"A brick once fell on my head. Haven't been the same since."

"BUDDIES"

17. Bows

"Don't you just love me?!"

18. Telebone

"Call me. We'll do lunch."

19. Razz

"Just put your lips together, stick out your tongue, and blow."

20. King Bones

"Welcome to my kingdom."

"BUDDIES"

21. Sheriff Bones

"I want you out of this book by sundown."

22. Rascal

"Trouble is my business."

23. Big Foot

"Could I borrow a pair of socks?"

24. Stinky

"Watch out, that's tear gas!"

"BUDDIES"

25. Baby

"Goo-goo, ga-ga."

26. Orbit

"People think I'm a little dizzy."

27. Skipper

"Anybody want to go on a three-hour tour?"

28. Zowie

"Have you met my friend Wow?"

"BUDDIES"

29. Nag

"Clean your room, make your bed, do your homework, yadda, yadda, yadda!"

30. Sharky

"Trust me."

31. Tentacle

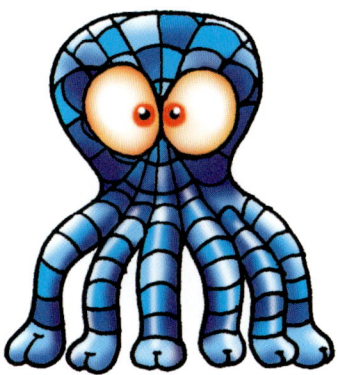

"Six legs, eight legs, what's the difference?"

32. Slack

"I hope to work one day. That's right — just one day."

"BUDDIES"

33. Matey

"There she blows—
her nose!"

34. Time Out

"You've been very,
very naughty."

35. Fly Boy

"Up, up, and away.
It's Super Bone!"

36. Rock Star

"I want my MTV!"

"BUDDIES"

37. Siesta

"I snooze, you lose."

38. Blades

"Sure beats walking."

39. Rat Fink

"Why doesn't anyone love me?"

40. Bone Boy

"What can I say? I just love milk!"

"BUDDIES"

41. Prep

"Aren't I perfect? You can call me Brad."

42. Liberty

"Man, this torch is heavy."

43. Stretch

"Yawn."

44. Timid

"Er, uh, I...er, never mind."

"BUDDIES"

45. Handy

"I can fix anything — unless, of course, it's broken."

46. Florence

"I'll nurse you back to health."

47. Puppy

"Guess what? I just made a mess in the kitchen."

48. Buck

"I don't think they're too big. Do you think they're too big?"

"BUDDIES"

49. Chatter

"I'm not scared.
I'm just keeping my
teeth warm."

50. Tie Dye

"Told you I'd be
back in style!"

51. Barney

"Safety first.
Always buckle up!"

52. Grammy

"I had to walk 9,000
miles to school—
without shoes!"

"BUDDIES"

53. Fish Bowl

"Desperate for attention? You bet!"

54. Hunchbone

"I just visited my cousin at Notre Dame."

55. Slick

"There's a little bridge I'd like to sell you."

56. Hiss

"Care for a bite?"

"BUDDIES"

57. Hulk

"My arms are my biggest charms."

58. Bookworm

"If you want to succeed, you've got to read!"

"MUTANTS"

62. The Fly

65. Jaws

Watch out for a special limited edition of "Mutants." It's some of your favorite characters

68. Sweetie

63. Monster

Coming soon to a Crazy Bones® pack near you!

THE ALIEN

They're creepy! They're crawly! And

"Dang! This may be a job for Sheriff Bones."

"Far out!"

SPECIAL REPORT!

This just in. Reports confirm that Aliens and Space Monsters have invaded Planet Go-Go. Why are they here? What do they want? No one knows for sure. Fortunately, we do have one eyewitness with us in the studio....

I know you guys think I'm nutty—and, well, hey, I AM Nutty—but I saw what I saw. I was inside a pack of Crazy Bones "Things." Suddenly I heard these strange noises. Then I saw a bright, glowing light. And there it was, an Alien from Outer Space. I was so scared, I bolted.

THESE AMAZING PICTURES WERE TAKEN BY OUR STAR PHOTOGRAPHER, FLASH, JUST MOMENTS AGO...

"ALIENS"

1. Salad Head

2. Brutus

3. Broom Head

4. Bikini Baby

5. Kanga

6. Fish Stick

"ALIENS"

7. Koalien

8. Tux

9. Nordic

10. Ar Ar

11. Chachee

12. Java

13. Pancho

"ALIENS"

14. Karate

15. Dragon

16. Duba Duba

17. Thinker

18. Gorbie

19. Boris

"ALIENS"

20. Kicker

21. Tropic

22. Bird Brain

23. Prince

24. 4x4

25. Bongo

26. Tarzalien

"ALIENS"

27. Statue

28. Squawk

29. Venus

30. Knight

31. Napo

32. Mona

33. Liberty

"ALIENS"

34. Super Go-Go

35. Rudolph

36. Schnoz

37. Cleo

38. Sphinx

39. Mumma Mia

"ALIENS"

40. Tut

41. Lips

42. Fido

44. Cyclops

43. Beard

45. Bone Dog

46. Claws

"ALIENS"

47. Stinky

48. Cyber
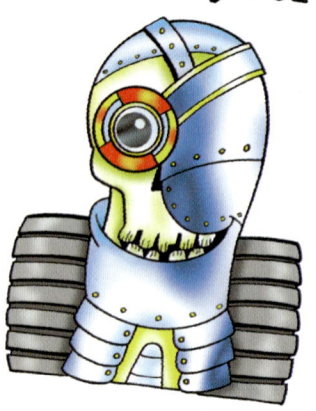

49. Rad Racer
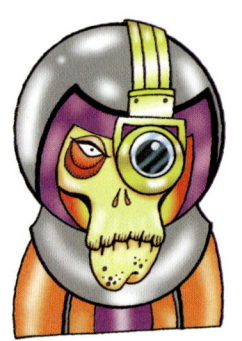

50. Martian

51. Tri-Clops

52. Bug Eye

53. Brain
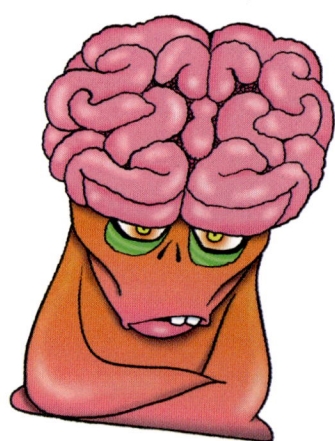

"ALIENS"

54. Moo

55. Space Frog

56. Creature

57. Lucas

58. Floss

59. Lagoon

60. Attila

PLAY CRAZY GAMES!

Okay. You can't sit around and stare at your Crazy Bones forever! Right?! After all, forever is a *loooong* time. So get up and start playing! Because the best part about Crazy Bones is all the games you can play with them!

Traditional

Each player takes turns to roll or throw five Crazy Bones into the air at the same time. You score points depending on how your Crazy Bones land.

Standing Up (Ace)	5
On Side	2
Face Up	1
Face Down	0

The winner is the person who scores the most points after three throws.

Bowling

Each player puts the same number of Crazy Bones on the ground. Place the Crazy Bones approximately six inches from a wall. Each player takes turns throwing a Crazy Bone and trying to knock down as many Crazy Bones as possible. Remember, the Crazy Bones must be thrown, not rolled. Each Crazy Bone you knock down that belongs to another player is worth one point. If you knock over one of your own Crazy Bones, you do not score. Just put it back in its original position. The winner is the player who has the most points after three throws.

On the Line

Draw a straight line on the ground or use a line that is already there. Each player throws a Crazy Bone—no rolling! The player whose Crazy Bone ends up closest to the line is the winner. The game can go on for as long as you like, provided that everyone throws the same number of times. The winner is the player with the most points.

Battle

One player lines up six Crazy Bones with a distance of approximately six inches between them. The second player does the same at a distance of about six feet from the other player. Flick a Crazy Bone and try to knock down the other player's Crazy Bones. Remove the Crazy Bones from the battlefield as they are knocked down. Each player takes the same number of turns. The winner is the player who knocks down the most Crazy Bones.

The Bomber

Each player places the same number of Crazy Bones inside a large circle. Players take turns throwing their Crazy Bones from a distance of about six feet, trying to knock the other players' Crazy Bones out of the circle. Each player takes the same number of turns. If you knock one of your own Crazy Bones out of the circle by mistake, it cannot be replaced. If you knock over a Crazy Bone but it does not fall out of the circle, you may stand it up again inside the circle. The winner is the player who has the highest number of his own Crazy Bones left inside the circle at the end of the game.

Airbone

Each player lines up five Crazy Bones at a distance of approximately two inches apart. Throw the first Crazy Bone into the air, quickly try to pick up the second Crazy Bone, and catch the first one before it falls. If you are able to do this, replace the second Crazy Bone and repeat the action with the third Crazy Bone, and so on. Next you throw the first Crazy Bone in the air and try to pick up two Crazy Bones at the same time before the first one falls. After that, throw the first Crazy Bone again, try to pick up a minimum of three Crazy Bones, and catch the first one before it falls. When a player makes a mistake, another player takes a turn. The winner is the first player to complete the game.

Basket

Place a cardboard box on the ground (an empty shoe box works best) about ten feet away from you. Each player takes turns trying to get a Crazy Bone into the box. But…the Crazy Bone must bounce at least once before it goes into the box. If you are really, really good you can decide that the Crazy Bone must bounce two or three times before it goes in. Each player can throw ten Crazy Bones each turn. The winner is the person who gets the most Crazy Bones into the box in ten throws.

Baseball

Create a baseball diamond by placing a Crazy Bone on first, second, and third base. Roll four Crazy Bones. Either four facing up or one standing up is a home run. Three facing up is a triple. Two facing up is a double. And one facing up is a single. All other combinations are outs.

Crazy Bone Chase

Two players each take one Crazy Bone and throw it in different directions. Taking turns, each player flicks their Crazy Bone at their opponent's Crazy Bone until one of the players hits the other Crazy Bone (tag, you win).

Crazy Bones Bone Roll

Find a flat surface such as a book or cookie sheet. Arrange the flat surface at an angle (propped up against a wall). Each player holds their Crazy Bone at the top of the angled flat surface and releases it. The player whose Crazy Bone is the first to reach the bottom is the winner.

Crazy Score

Take three Crazy Bones in your hand and toss them in the air. After they have landed, determine which player goes first. That player must flick one of the Crazy Bones between the other two. This is called scoring. Then the next person takes a turn. The object of the game is to make it as difficult as possible for the other person to score by leaving as narrow a passage as possible for your opponent to score a goal.

Use your Own Crazy Brains...
and invent your own games!

You can create lots of other ways to play with your Crazy Bones. Ask your mom, dad, or grandparents for ideas from games they played when they were your age. The number of different games you can play is as boundless as your imagination! Go crazy!

THE END!